THE NIGHT SHIMMY

This is a Borzoi Book published by Alfred A. Knopf, Inc.

Text copyright © 1991 Gwen Strauss.
Illustrations copyright © 1991 A.E.T. Browne & Partners.
All rights reserved under International and Pan-American Copyright Conventions.
Published in the United States by Alfred A. Knopf, Inc., New York.
Distributed by Random House, Inc., New York. Originally published in Great Britain
by Julia MacRae Books, an imprint of the Random Century Group.

First American Edition, 1992

Printed in Hong Kong
10   9   8   7   6   5   4   3   2   1

Library of Congress Cataloging-in-Publication Data
Strauss, Gwen.
The Night Shimmy / written by Gwen Strauss ; illustrated by
Anthony Browne.—1st American ed.   p.   cm.
Summary: Eric would rather spend time with his imaginary companion
the Night Shimmy than socialize with others, until the day he makes
an unexpected friend in the park.
ISBN 0-679-82384-0 (trade)   ISBN 0-679-92384-5 (lib. bdg.)
[1. Imaginary playmates—Fiction.   2. Friendship—Fiction.]
I. Browne, Anthony, ill.   II. Title.   PZ7.S91236Ni   1992
[E]—dc20   91-11294

THE NIGHT SHIMMY

Gwen Strauss & Anthony Browne

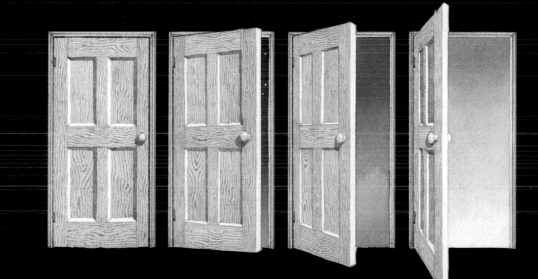

Eric did not like to talk.
Other children didn't understand why.
They called him "Dumb Eric".
They teased him with silly questions:
"What's the matter? Cat got your tongue?"
Grown-ups asked him if he was shy.
But Eric didn't answer.

He just didn't like talking.

And anyway he didn't have to talk
because his secret friend, the Night Shimmy, spoke for him.
The Night Shimmy explained why Eric couldn't
eat his peas, or why he didn't need a bath.

The Night Shimmy always chose the best stories
to read before Eric went to sleep.
And if Eric had frightening lizard dreams,
the Night Shimmy shooed their flicking tongues

When Eric's father asked, "What would you like for breakfas[t]
the Night Shimmy said, "Porridge, please,
with loads of milk and honey."
Just the way Eric liked it best.

The Night Shimmy could be invisible, see in the dark,
and speak in the language of Shimmy, which only Eric and the
Night Shimmy knew. The Night Shimmy was also an expert spy.
He could hear the smallest sounds... a creak on the stairs

...or the crack of a kite in the sky.
Marcia was playing in the park.
She caught them spying.
She didn't care that Eric was quiet.
She didn't ask him silly questions, or try to
make him talk, or call him "Dumb Eric".
Even the Night Shimmy didn't have to say a word.

Marcia and Eric climbed the apple tree and
swung around like monkeys.
Eric made gorilla noises.

They flew Marcia's parrot.
It hung in the sky until the sky lost almost all its colour.
Then Marcia said goodnight, and Eric ran all the way home.

He ate his peas, had a bath, and went to bed.
That night he didn't dream of lizards.

When he woke up the Night Shimmy was not there.
Eric searched under the covers, in drawers, in cupboards,
and in all of their secret hide-outs.
His mother asked, "What's the matter, dear?
Why are you stomping about?"
But Eric pressed his mouth tight shut.
Under the bed he whispered,
"Night Shimmy, are you there?"

Eric stayed in bed until
his father called three times.
All day long he thumped and kicked things

Marcia came to the front door. He heard her ask,
"Would Eric like to play with me?"

Eric stood at the window. He watched Marcia trying to fly her kite.
It stuttered up, just a little bit, but when the wind died it fell and
tangled in a tree.   Then Eric knew what he could do. He went
outside and took a deep breath.
"I can get your kite," he told Marcia.

All on his own he climbed to the very top and freed the kite.

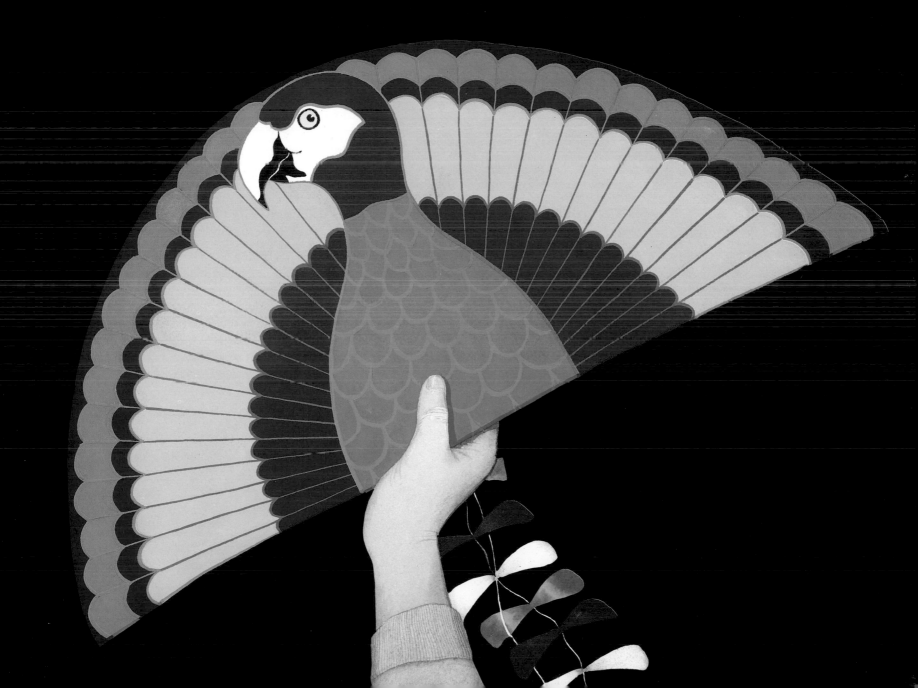

They began to talk.
Eric found he had many things to say.

When a breeze came up, they flew Marcia's kite
until the first stars came out. They made silent wishes.
Then Eric said, "Goodnight."

And the Night Shimmy waved.